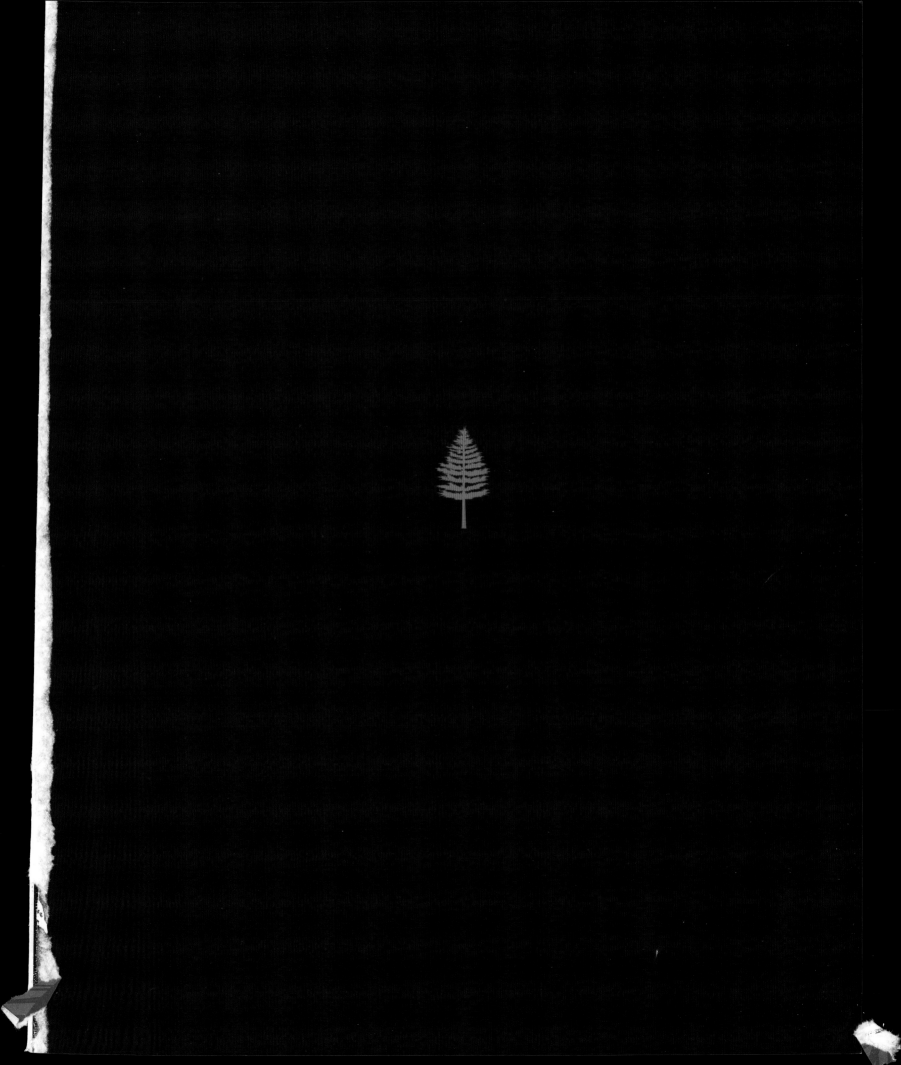

I would like to dedicate this book to the people who helped shape me:

To my most treasured friend, Sarah Floyd. Thank you for delving deep and unearthing the diamond in the rough. I wouldn't be where I am without your invaluable wisdom and support. I am blessed to call you my friend.

To my 7th grade teacher, colleague, and personal hero, Mrs. Carol Quinney. Your love and support during a very difficult time in my life is what led me to discover my inner worth. Thank you for protecting, encouraging, and inspiring me. You'll always hold a special place in my heart.

A special thank-you to my fantastic agent, Rebecca Angus. Thank you for taking a chance on me. We make a great team, and I am so thankful you're on this journey with me.

Last, but certainly not least . . . my family. There are too many of you to list, so here's an Irish thank-you (yes, I just made that up). If you're reading this, I love you. Thank you for supporting me in every way possible!

FAMILIUS

Published by Familius LLC.
1254 Commerce Way, Sanger, CA 93657.
www.familius.com

Familius books are available at special discounts for bulk purchases, whether for sales promotions or for family or corporate use. For more information, contact Familius Sales at 559-876-2170 or email orders@familius.com. Reproduction of this book in any manner, in whole or in part, without written permission of the publisher is prohibited.

LIBRARY OF CONGRESS CATALOGING-IN-PUBLICATION DATA
2019903658   ISBN 9781641701587   eISBN 9781641702089

Printed in China

Edited by Kaylee Mason and Brooke Jorden
Book and jacket design by David Miles and Derek George

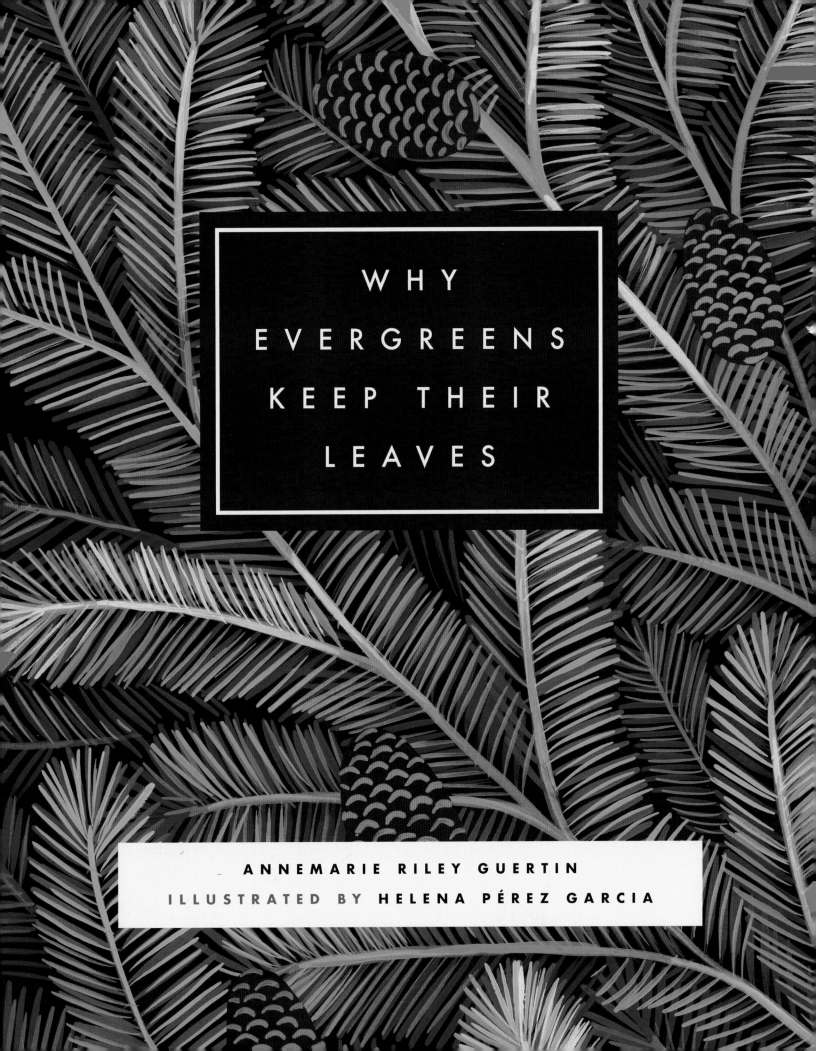

WHY EVERGREENS KEEP THEIR LEAVES

ANNEMARIE RILEY GUERTIN

ILLUSTRATED BY HELENA PÉREZ GARCIA

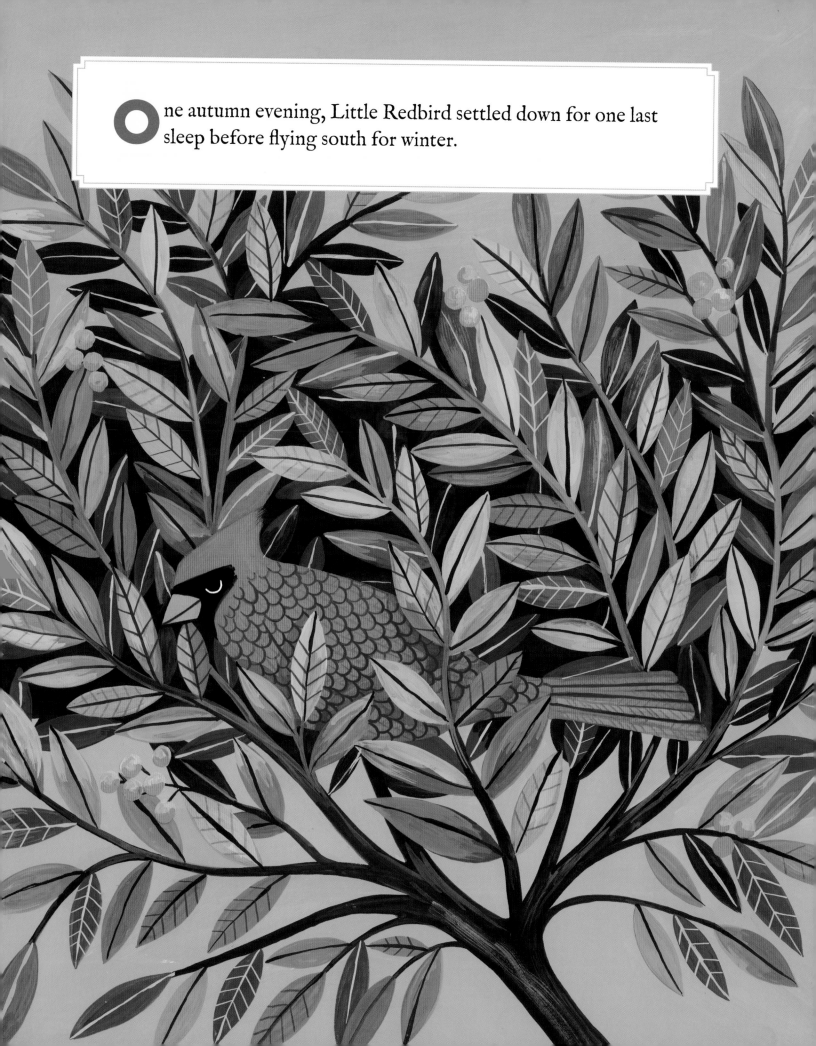

One autumn evening, Little Redbird settled down for one last sleep before flying south for winter.

As she slept, a strong gust of wind shook her from her cozy nest in the eaves of the barn. Little Redbird tumbled out and fell onto the cold, hard ground.

"Ouch!" she cried as she stretched out her wing. "I will not be able to fly south with this injured wing. How will I survive the long, harsh winter winds? Surely I will perish."

As the sun rose, Little Redbird spotted the tall, strong trees of the forest. She chirped with relief. "One of those trees will make a fine home for the winter! Its leaves will shield me from the wind, and I shall build a new nest on a low, sturdy branch."

Gathering her strength, Little Redbird hopped and fluttered into the forest.

The first tree she came upon was a silvery-white birch.

"Beautiful birch tree," she said, "I have fallen and injured my wing. May I live in your warm branches until spring returns?"

"My goodness!" said the birch. "It's hard enough for me to stand against the bitter winds. I can't be bothered trying to keep you safe as well. Now move along!"

Little Redbird fluttered on until she came to a large oak tree.

"Good morning, strong oak tree," Little Redbird called. "I have fallen and hurt my wing. May I live in your branches until spring returns?"

"Oh my!" exclaimed the oak tree. "If I let you stay in my branches then you might ask me for some of my acorns. I work hard to make them, and I can't have you eating them all up. Go away; I have work to do before winter arrives."

So Little Redbird fluttered on until
she came upon a hardy maple tree.
"Hardy maple tree," Little
Redbird cried, "I have fallen and
injured my wing. May I live in your
branches until spring returns?"

"No," he replied, "I am too busy making sap for maple syrup. I have no time for little birds. Be on your way!"

Poor Little Redbird didn't know what to do. Tears as big as raindrops streamed down her cheeks.

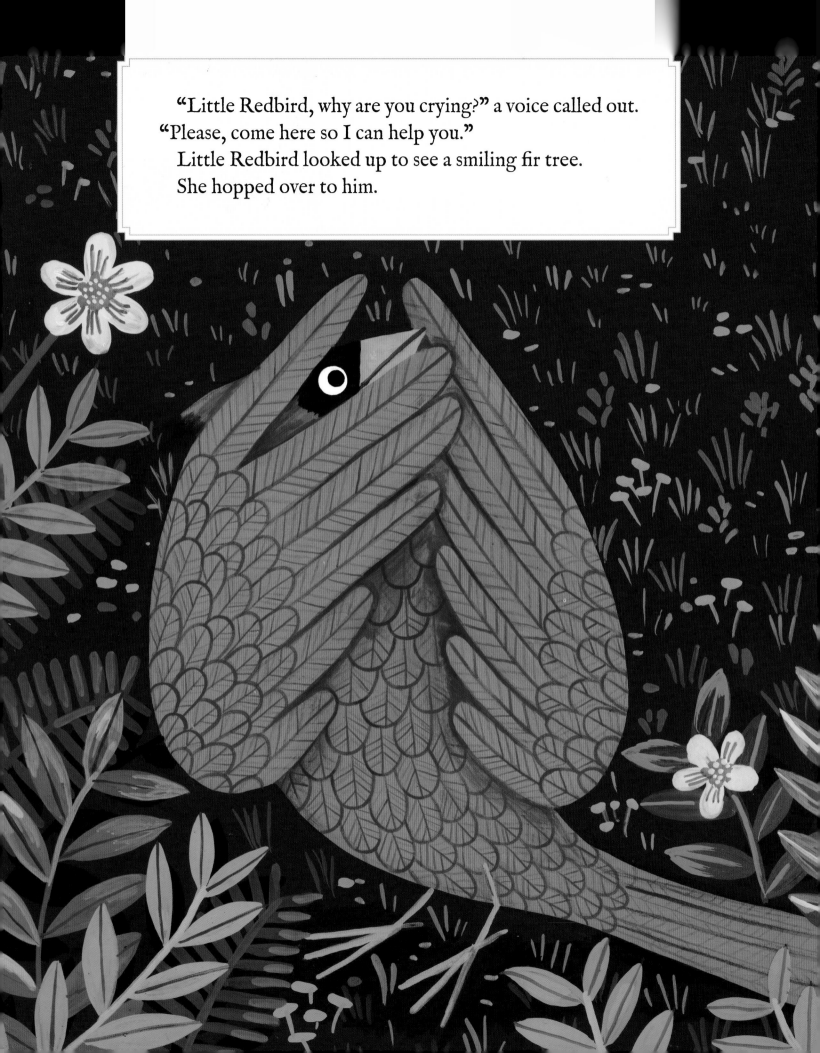

"Little Redbird, why are you crying?" a voice called out.
"Please, come here so I can help you."
Little Redbird looked up to see a smiling fir tree.
She hopped over to him.

"Oh, fir tree," Little Redbird said, "I have fallen and hurt my wing. I am looking for a place to keep warm for winter, but I have no place to go."

"No place to go?" he asked. "Why, I have plenty of room in my branches if you'd like to stay with me. I will keep you safe and warm."

"Thank you!" cried Little Redbird. "But I don't have the strength to fly up to your branches."
"Worry no more," he replied.

"I'm happy to help too," a voice called out.
Standing tall beside the fir tree was a beautiful blue spruce.

"My branches are strong. I will shield you from the cold north wind," he said.

"How kind of you!" replied Little Redbird.

"I will care for you too," a lovely voice whispered through the pines.

"I may be small, but I make big, juicy berries all winter long," said the juniper tree. "My berries will help heal you."

So, Little Redbird built a warm nest inside the fir tree's branches and waited for winter's arrival.

Not long afterward, the Frost Queen and her son, Jack, were out on an evening stroll through the forest.

"Mother, may I touch the leaves on every tree in the forest?" Jack asked.

"No, Jack," his mother replied. "See those three trees?" she said as she pointed. "They were very kind to one of my precious birds who had injured her wing. They gave her a place to rest and food to eat."

"You may touch the leaves on every tree in the forest except for the fir, spruce, and juniper. They may keep their green leaves all year round," she replied. "And they shall forevermore be called evergreen."

So, it is said, because of their act of kindness, not only do the fir, spruce, and juniper trees get to keep their leaves in winter, but the red birds stay all winter long to keep them company.